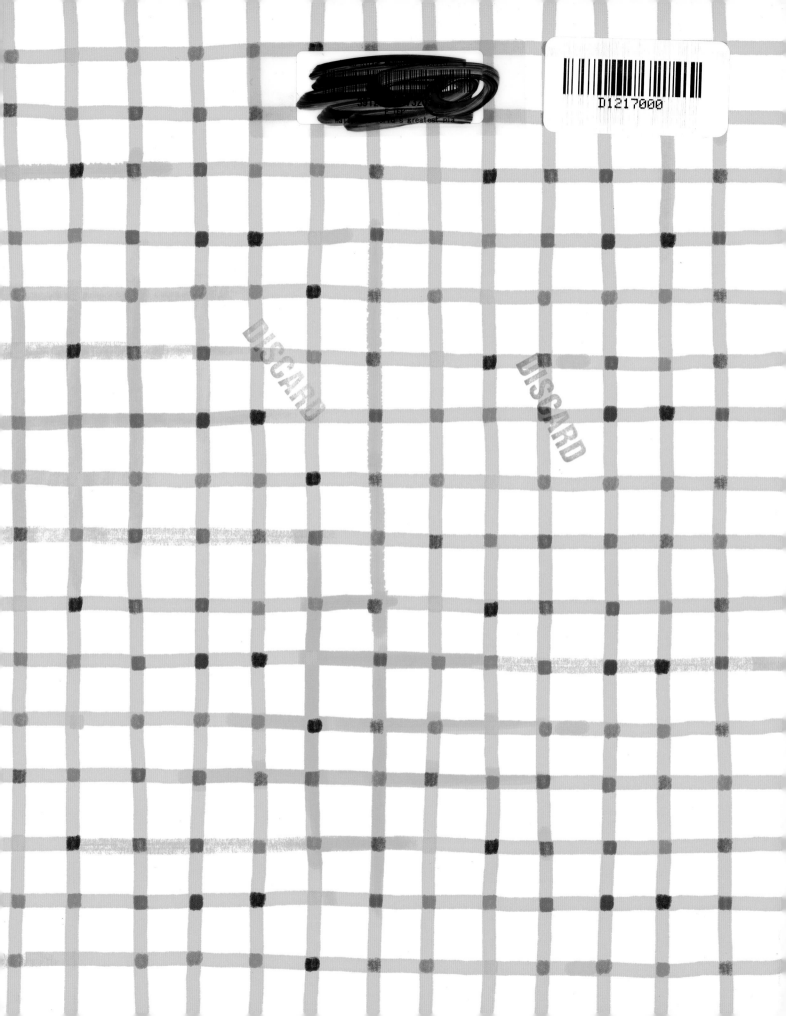

**FOR CLAIRE AND SOPHIE** —*Ratha*

**FOR M. O.** —*Camilla*

Published by
Princeton Architectural Press
70 West 36th Street
New York, NY 10018
www.papress.com

Printed and bound in China
25 24 23 22   4 3 2 1 First Edition

ISBN: 978-1-64896-180-9

Published by arrangement with Debbie Bibo Agency

Editors: Rob Shaeffer and Parker Menzimer
Design: Camilla Pintonato
Layout: Natalie Snodgrass

Library of Congress Control Number: 2022933189

Ratha Tep Camilla Pintonato

# WALLY
## *the* WORLD'S GREATEST
## Piano-Playing
## WOMBAT

Princeton Architectural Press · New York

Wally Wombat loved to play the piano.

Under the towering eucalyptus tree,
his paws danced over the keys and his
heart soared.

Wally became the

**WORLD'S GREATEST
PIANO-PLAYING**

wombat!

Until he realized
**HE WASN'T.**

So Wally practiced
and became the
**WORLD'S GREATEST
TAP-DANCING,
PIANO-PLAYING**
wombat.

Until he realized

**HE WASN'T.**

Wally kept practicing
and became the

**WORLD'S GREATEST
BALL-TWIRLING,
TAP-DANCING,
PIANO-PLAYING**
wombat.

Until he realized
**HE WASN'T.**

# "ENOUGH!"

Wally erupted.
He was frustrated.

As hard as he'd tried,
he hadn't been the greatest.

Wally covered up his piano and retreated into his burrow. If he couldn't be the greatest, he wouldn't play at all.

Wally kept busy. He read books, picked up knitting,
and got a pet. But he missed doing what he loved most.

One night Wally awoke to a rustling.
He peered outside.

It was the other wombat! And he
was lurking around Wally's piano!
Surely he was up to no good.

Wally rushed over before the other wombat
could do any harm.

"Hi," the other wombat said.
"Care for a cookie?"

Wally was flustered. Was this a picnic?

"I'm Wylie, by the way. I was hoping you'd
come back. I miss playing the piano with
you."

Wally wasn't sure what to think.

"You miss playing with me?"

"Of course! You made playing the piano
so fun," said Wylie. "And you made me try
harder, so I played better."

Wally blushed. He'd never thought of it
that way. He supposed that Wylie had made
him play better, too.

The two wombats had chocolate chip cookies and milk.

And they played a duet on the piano.

Then they came up with a plan.

The
**WORLD'S**
**GREATEST**
plan.

They practiced...

...and had more chocolate chip cookies and milk.

And practiced some more.

Finally, they were ready.

AH

OOOH

The audience *oohed* and *aahed* beneath the towering stage, then gasped and cheered as the duo walked out.

AAH

OH!

Wally and Wylie were,
without a doubt, the
**WORLD'S GREATEST
BLINDFOLDED,
UNICYCLING,
FLAMETHROWING,
HULA-HOOPING,
PIANO-PLAYING**
wombats ever!

Until they realized
**THEY WEREN'T.**